My Dad is G
But He Will be Back ...y!

A Deployment Story

Deployment Series
Book 1

James R. Thomas

Dedication

This book is dedicated to the military service members serving our country and their families supporting them. We serve together!

My dad is going away, but he will be back one day. Before he leaves, I will give him a big hug and a kiss, so big I cannot miss. My dad is going away on a trip, something he cannot skip.

While my dad is away, my mom will take care of me each day. Everything will be all right, since my mom will be with me day and night. She's here to help out, without any doubt, so there's no need for me to pout.

When my dad is gone, my mom can take me to the park, as long as it's not dark. I can go play on the slide—boy what a ride! I can swing really high, making me feel like I can fly! The great thing is that while my mom is here, there's no need to have any fear.

When my dad is away, I can write letters to him each day. I will have a lot of things to write, much to his delight.

Dear Dad,

I miss you and I cannot wait to see you.

Love,

(your name)

I can send my letters through the mail—that will travel by boat, air, or rail. My dad will be happy to read my letters, which will make him feel better. Or I can send e-mails through the internet, which will travel faster than a jet. Whichever way I write, it will be all right.

I will also receive letters from my dad through e-mail or by post mail, hopefully telling me a short story or a tale. He sometimes likes to use and mail colorful paper letters, which I think is a lot better.

Dear (your name),

I miss you and hope to see you soon. I love getting mailed letters and e-mails from you.

Love,

Dad

While my dad is away, I can draw lots of colorful pictures for him. We talk about each one, particularly the one with the smiling sun. I like to draw all the time, but mostly before my bedtime.

My dad told me he would send me some pictures of the places he has seen. I think that would be very keen. Maybe I can send him some pictures too! I have some of me in a canoe. But don't forget the one with me in the sun, where I'm having so much fun.

When my dad calls me on the phone to say hello, my face will really glow. I can tell him what I have done, while he has been gone. I have so much to say that my mom told me there's not enough time in each day. So, I tell my dad my favorite part, straight from the heart.

My dad might call during the day or at night. Anytime will be all right! I just want to hear his voice, so I can rejoice. Each time I can't wait, and boy is his voice great!

My dad is coming back soon and should be home today around noon. We have made him a welcome home sign, so I cannot wait until it's time.

Today my dad came home from his trip, something he could not skip. And now since he is back, he has to unpack. I knew my dad would be back one day, and now we can go play. Hooray!

THE END

Cut Here

Dear _____,

_____

_____

_____

_____

_____

_____

_____

_____

_____

Love,

_____

Draw a picture here.

C
u
t

H
e
r
e

Dear _____,

_____

_____

_____

_____

_____

_____

_____

_____

_____

Love,

_____

Draw a picture here.

ABOUT THE AUTHOR

James R. Thomas takes young readers into the world of space travel, teaches them the importance of conservation, and also tackles the topic of helping children cope when a parent is deployed in the military. His writing style has been inspired by his military service and the challenges his own family faced with his deployment. He also wants to bring his love of science fiction to life for children and teach them to be socially conscious of our planet.

In his books, he addresses a variety of life issues for young readers with his goal being to help children build an awareness of the world around them and to empower them to reach for the stars. Through his character, Joe Devlin, children can explore space travel of the future in the intergalactic world of the Space Academy series. The series was inspired when James was being deployed to Afghanistan and promised to write a story for his son, which Joe Devlin was based upon. James's conservation series teaches children the importance of keeping our planet healthy and safe while showing them that every single person, including the reader, can make an impact on the planet, good or bad. Included in the eighteen books that James has published thus far are two stand-alones. One covers the importance of telling the truth and the other teaches children about allergies.

James also has expanded internationally with a children's book published in the French language. To round out his versatility as an author, he tapped into his own life experiences and crafted a series to help children cope with the deployment of a loved one.

James is a graduate of the United States Naval Academy with a bachelor of science in aerospace engineering, and he holds an advanced degree in business administration. He is married with a son and a daughter and resides in Chesapeake, Virginia. When he is not writing, he enjoys spending time with his family, playing guitar, and flying.

For more books by James R. Thomas

Space Academy Series
Joe Devlin: And New Star Fighter
Joe Devlin: And the Lost Star Fighter
Joe Devlin: In the Moon's Shadow
Joe Devlin: At the Enemy's Hand

Deployment Series
My Dad is Going Away But He Will be Back One Day
My Mom is Going Away But She Will be Back One Day
What Will I Play While You Are Away?
We're Moving Today!

Conservation Series
Boy Does Trash Fly!
Boy Does Water Run!
Boy Does Electricity Glow!
Boy Are Animals Wild!

Visit James R. Thomas paperbacks on the World Wide Web at
https://sites.google.com/site/childrenpicturebooks/

Made in the USA
Middletown, DE
11 December 2019